Dear Parents:

Congratulations! Your child is taking the first steps on an exciting journey. The destination? Independent reading!

STEP INTO READING® will help your child get there. The program offers five steps to reading success. Each step includes fun stories and colorful art or photographs. In addition to original fiction and books with favorite characters, there are Step into Reading Non-Fiction Readers, Phonics Readers and Boxed Sets, Sticker Readers, and Comic Readers—a complete literacy program with something to interest every child.

Learning to Read, Step by Step!

Ready to Read   Preschool–Kindergarten
• big type and easy words • rhyme and rhythm • picture clues
For children who know the alphabet and are eager to begin reading.

Reading with Help   Preschool–Grade 1
• basic vocabulary • short sentences • simple stories
For children who recognize familiar words and sound out new words with help.

Reading on Your Own   Grades 1–3
• engaging characters • easy-to-follow plots • popular topics
For children who are ready to read on their own.

Reading Paragraphs   Grades 2–3
• challenging vocabulary • short paragraphs • exciting stories
For newly independent readers who read simple sentences with confidence.

Ready for Chapters   Grades 2–4
• chapters • longer paragraphs • full-color art
For children who want to take the plunge into chapter books but still like colorful pictures.

STEP INTO READING® is designed to give every child a successful reading experience. The grade levels are only guides; children will progress through the steps at their own speed, developing confidence in their reading.

Remember, a lifetime love of reading starts with a single step!

Step into Reading, Random House, and the Random House colophon are registered trademarks of Penguin Random House LLC.

Visit us on the Web!
StepIntoReading.com
randomhousekids.com

Educators and librarians, for a variety of teaching tools, visit us at RHTeachersLibrarians.com

ISBN 978-0-7364-3498-0 (trade) — ISBN 978-0-7364-8231-8 (lib. bdg.)
ISBN 978-0-7364-3499-7 (ebook)

Printed in the United States of America   10 9 8 7 6 5 4 3 2

Disney · PIXAR
FINDING
DORY

DORY'S STORY

by Bill Scollon

illustrated by the Disney Storybook Art Team

Random House New York

Dory is
a little fish.

She has trouble
with her memory.

Dory does not remember
how to get home.
She is lost.
She asks
everyone she
meets for help.

No one knows
where Dory lives.

Dory becomes friends
with Nemo and Marlin.
They all live together
in a coral reef.

One day, Dory remembers
a place called
the Jewel of Morro Bay.
Maybe her home is there!

Dory crosses the ocean
with Nemo and Marlin
to find her home.
She gets stuck
in a plastic ring!

Dory gets taken to
the Jewel of Morro Bay.
It is a big aquarium!

Nemo and Marlin
want to find Dory.
A bird carries them
into the aquarium!

Dory meets an octopus.

His name is Hank.

He helps Dory figure out

where her parents live.

Dory finds her home.
Her parents are gone.
A crab says they went
to the hospital.

The pipes will take Dory
to the hospital.

Destiny is a whale shark.

Bailey is a beluga.

They show Dory the way.

Nemo and Marlin
find Dory in the pipe.
They swim off together
to find Dory's parents.

Dory's parents are not at
the fish hospital.

Dory falls
down a drain!
The drain drops her
into the ocean.

Dory is alone.

She follows a shell path.

It leads her
to her parents!

Nemo and Marlin are
on a truck
with the hospital fish.
Dory will save them!

Becky helps rescue
Nemo and Marlin.
Dory is still
in the truck!

Hank scares
the truck driver away.
They drive off the pier
into the ocean!

The fish are happy
to return to the sea.
Destiny and Bailey
join them!

Dory's parents go
back to the reef
with Dory
and her friends.
They are all
one big happy family!